SITTING DUCKS

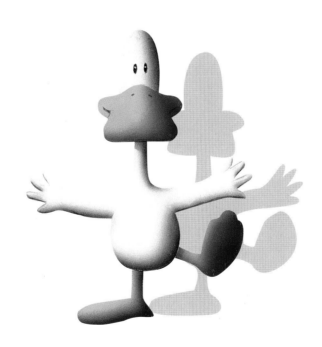

For Liz and Jean-Paul with much love.
And to my parents, Joe and Lee,
who planted seeds in all the
empty spaces in my head.

Special thanks to Bob Commander for coming to the rescue.

Copyright © 1998 by Michael Bedard. All rights reserved. Published by The Putnam & Grosset Group, a division of Penguin Putnam Books for Young Readers, New York. Published simultaneously in Canada. Printed in Hong Kong.

Library of Congress Cataloging-in-Publication Data

Bedard, Michael, 1949-
  Sitting ducks / by Michael Bedard.
    p. cm.
  Summary: A sympathetic alligator befriends a lonely duck and becomes alienated from the rest of the town's alligators who think of ducks only as food.
  [1. Ducks—Fiction. 2. Alligators—Fiction. 3. Friendship—Fiction.] I. Title
PZ7.B381798Si 1998
[E]—dc21
                                         97-50355
                                         CIP

ISBN 0-399-22847-0   C D E F G H I J   AC

SITTING DUCKS

Michael Bedard

PUTNAM & GROSSET
New York

Day after day, a steady supply of ducks rolled off the assembly line at the Colossal Duck Factory. Alligators pushed buttons and pulled levers that kept the machines humming, while conveyor belts moved the ducks through the factory. Finally, the ducks were loaded onto trucks for their journey to the city. Rarely did anything go wrong.

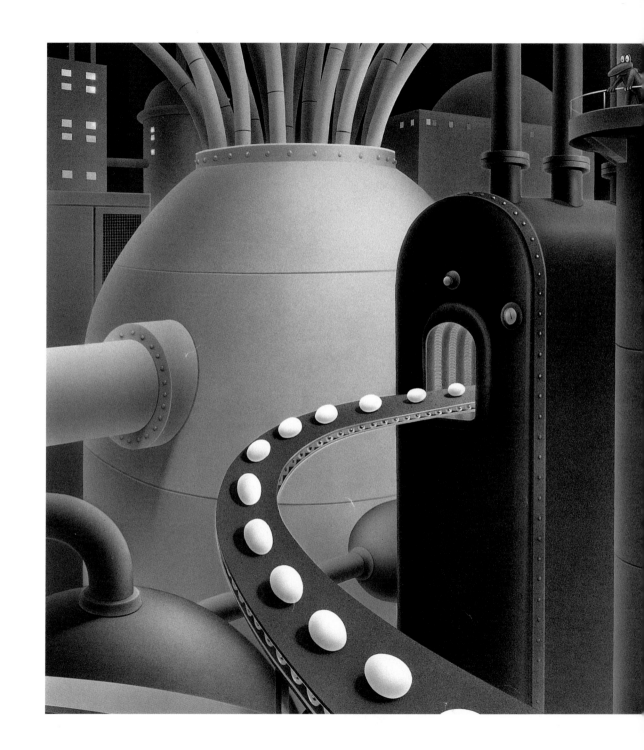

But one day, an egg came through the incubation chamber unhatched. It rolled off the assembly line and fell down, down, down into the shadowy darkness below.

The egg landed with a loud crack on the factory floor. Dazed by this rude introduction to the world, a little duck emerged and surveyed his strange surroundings.

He wandered through
the forest of machinery,
awed by its size and dazzled
by its beauty.

The next thing he knew, the little duck came face-to-face
with one of the worker alligators, who was very surprised
to see a duck wandering freely about the factory.

Instead of returning the little duck to the assembly line, the alligator stuffed him into his lunch pail . . .

... and left the factory.

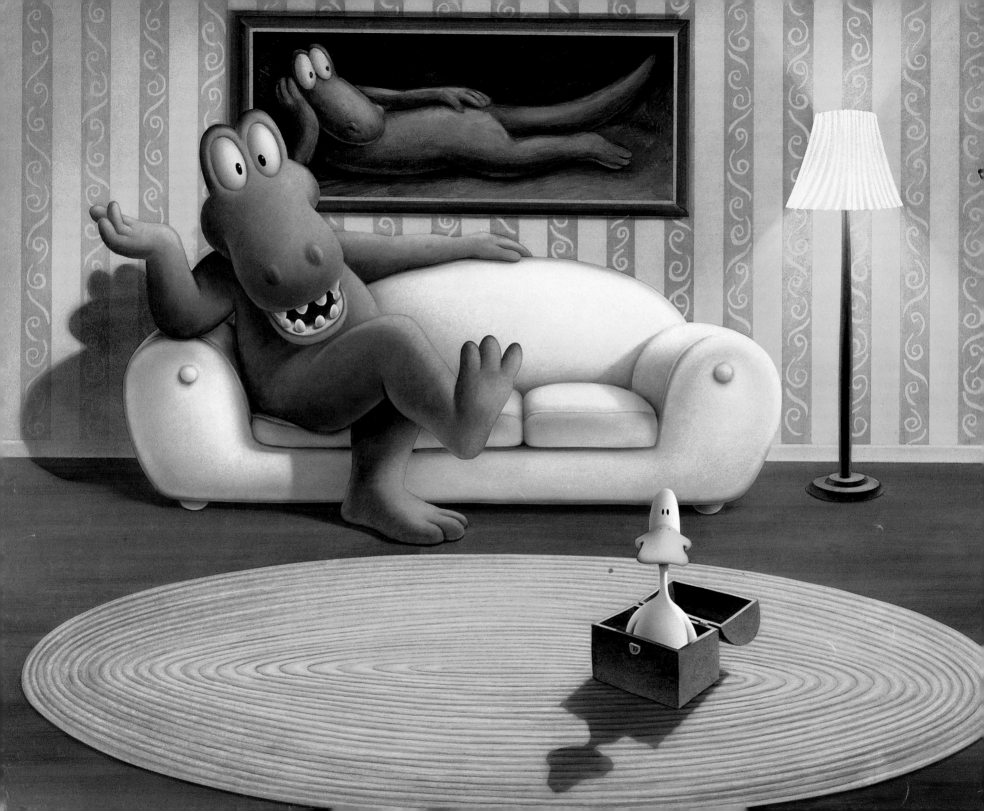

When the little duck emerged from the lunch pail, he found himself in a nicely decorated apartment. The alligator acted friendly, but all the while he was thinking what a delicious meal the duck would make when properly fattened.

Each day when the alligator went off to work, the little duck was left by himself with a large supply of tasty snacks. The days were long and lonely.

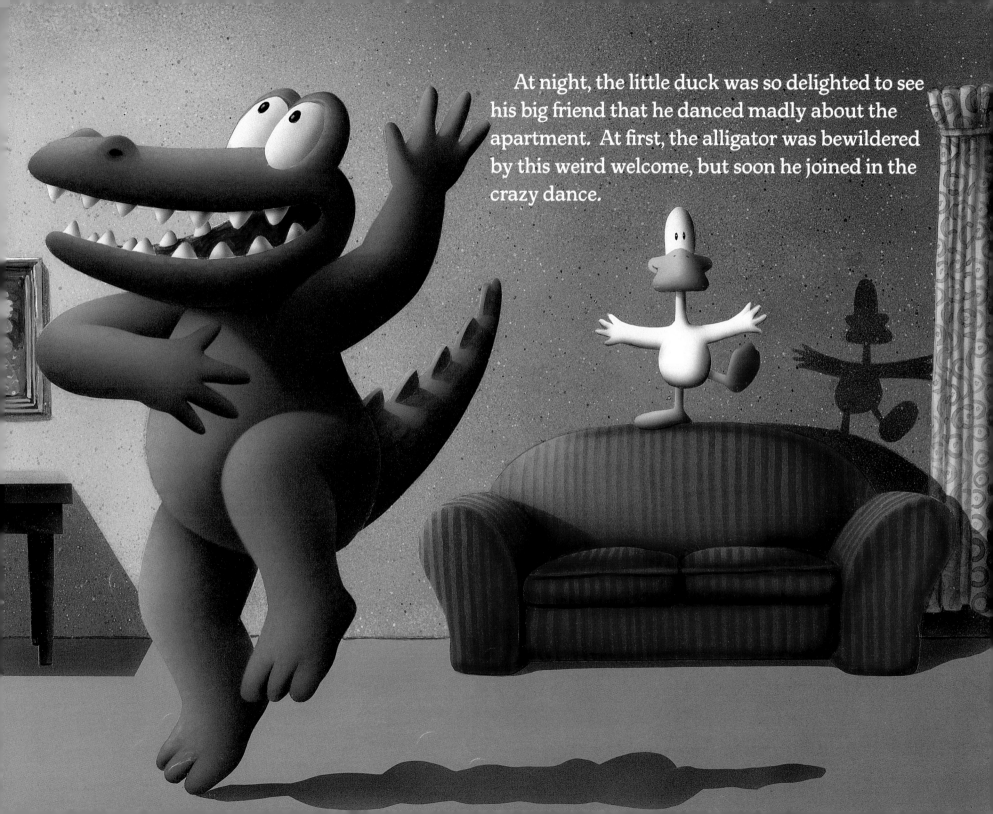

At night, the little duck was so delighted to see his big friend that he danced madly about the apartment. At first, the alligator was bewildered by this weird welcome, but soon he joined in the crazy dance.

As their friendship grew and grew, the alligator thought less and less about eating the little duck. They even tried going out together, but it proved to be very awkward.

One night, while the alligator worked late at the factory, the little duck pondered the world outside his window. The alligator had warned him never to venture out alone, but the duck's curiosity got the best of him. He just had to sneak away and explore the streets below.

Farther and farther
the little duck roamed,
until he was hopelessly
lost and very scared.

Rounding a corner, the little duck came upon a brightly lit diner. His heart leapt when he saw another duck inside. He rushed in and hopped up onto a stool.

"Boy, am I glad to see you," said the little duck breathlessly. "Do you have anything good to eat?"

"Oh, yes," said the waiter duck.

Up popped a huge alligator from behind the counter.
   "WE CERTAINLY DO!"

The little duck surely would have ended up in a stew if his alligator friend had not arrived just in time to rescue him.

Shaken and sleepless from their frightening experience, the duck and the alligator lay awake talking.

"I guess I owe you an explanation," said the alligator, and he went on to tell the terrible truth. "After the ducks are hatched at the factory, they are shipped to a part of the city called Ducktown. There they eat and eat until they grow so fat they can't fly away. Eventually, I'm afraid, they end up as the main course in our favorite restaurants."

"Ducks can fly?" asked the little duck. The alligator nodded. The duck was quiet for a while. Then he asked, "Will you take me to Ducktown? I have a plan."

The next day the alligator took the little duck to the edge of Ducktown.
It was very difficult for them to say good-bye.
"Don't worry," said the duck. "It's better this way. Trust me."

The little duck wasted no time in spreading the news. At first, nobody would believe his story about the alligators. They thought he was just a troublemaker. But when the little duck showed them the menu from the Decoy Cafe, the ducks were stunned.

"Listen," the little duck said, "this is what we have to do."

He told the ducks that if they exercised vigorously they would lose weight and become strong. Then they would be able to fly south, where they would be free and safe from the alligators.

Soon the sky was filled with flying ducks. After some practice, they were ready to fly south, just as ducks are supposed to do.

When the alligators looked up and saw their delicious ducks flying away, they were very angry. All except for one alligator, who was very sad.

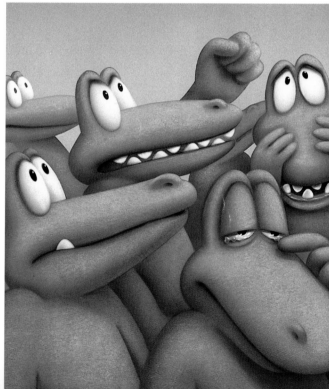

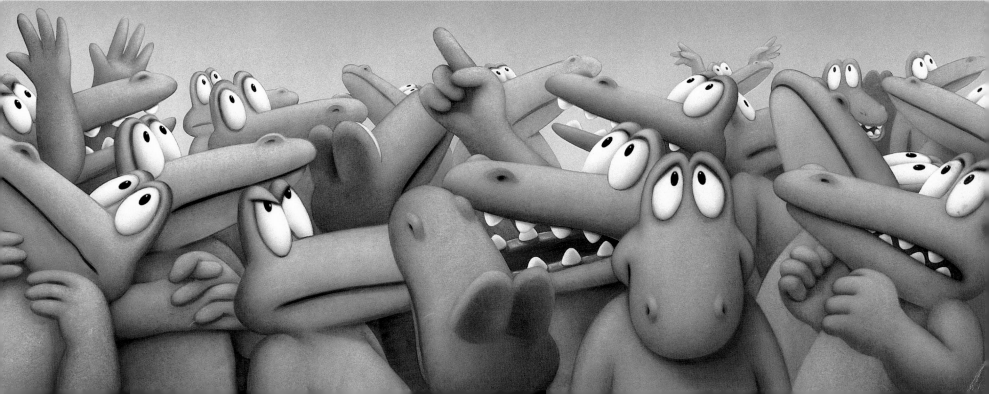

The alligator was sure he would never see his little friend again. But suddenly the duck burst into the apartment with two tickets in his hand.

"I couldn't leave without you."

So, together, they flew south.

The ducks followed the sun to a beautiful, tropical island. They were thrilled to find their little hero waiting for them, but they were very nervous about having an alligator in their midst. They needn't have worried, though. Mostly, the alligator passed the time dreaming about chicken. Life was good at the Flapping Arms Seaside Resort.